Cherri Greeno is a two-time National Newspaper Award winner who currently works as a corporate communications and public information expert in law enforcement.

Cherri was born and raised in Nova Scotia before moving to Ontario to pursue her Master of Arts in Journalism degree. She worked several years as a newspaper reporter before delving into the world of corporate communications and media relations.

She currently resides in Kitchener, Ontario with her most cherished accomplishments to date – her four beautiful, strong, smart, and witty daughters who are the inspiration behind her first-ever Children's book, *Mismatched Martha*.

MISMATCHED MARTHA

CHERRI GREENO

AUSTIN MACAULEY PUBLISHERS™
LONDON • CAMBRIDGE • NEW YORK • SHARJAH

Ordering Information
Quantity sales: Special discounts are available on quantity purchases by corporations, associations, and others. For details, contact the publisher at the address below.

Publisher's Cataloging-in-Publication data
Greeno, Cherri
Mismatched Martha

ISBN 9781649794789 (Paperback)
ISBN 9781649794796 (ePub e-book)

Library of Congress Control Number: 2022913775

www.austinmacauley.com/us

First Published 2022
Austin Macauley Publishers LLC
40 Wall Street, 33rd Floor, Suite 3302
New York, NY 10005
USA

mail-usa@austinmacauley.com
+1 (646) 5125767

I would like to thank my extraordinary and miraculous daughters for the inspiration behind *Mismatched Martha*. You made me realize, from the very moment you were born, that dreams do come true. I hope this book shows you the importance of never giving up, of continuing to dream big, and, most of all, to always walk your own path.

I would like to thank the team at Austin Macauley Publishers for their constant attention to detail throughout the editing, designing, production, and marketing process. Most of all, thank you for investing in *Mismatched Martha's* journey and for seeing the value in her message - that it is more than ok to be different. In fact, it's pretty magical.

Martha always knew she was different.
She liked to say silly sayings.

She liked to tell tantalizing tales.
But, most of all, Martha liked to wear
wacky wardrobes.

Socks were her favorite.
In fact, Martha made sure to match
her socks to whatever mood she was
feeling. But there was one exception.
The socks could never, ever match.
So. . .

On Monday morning, Martha woke up
feeling Merry. She always liked Monday
because Monday starts with the letter M,
just like her name.

She reached into her drawer and pulled
out the merriest socks she could find.

But when she got to school, she noticed that people were pointing and laughing. They thought her mismatched socks were silly.

But Martha loved her socks. And so, she walked through the playground proudly.

On Tuesday, Martha woke up
feeling Thankful.

She was thankful for all the wonderful and beautiful clothes she had-especially her socks.

She reached into her drawer and pulled out the socks she was most thankful for, the ones with all her favourite colors on them.

But when she got to school, she noticed that people were pointing and laughing. They thought her mismatched socks were silly.

But Martha loved her socks. And so, she walked through the playground proudly.

On Wednesday, Martha woke up feeling Wishful. She wished that people wouldn't laugh at her today.

She reached into her drawer and pulled out the most wishful socks she could, closing her eyes and wishing for a day where no one made fun of her.

But when she got to school, she noticed
people were pointing and laughing. They
thought her mismatched socks
were silly.

But Martha loved her socks.
But she didn't love being made fun of.
She hung her head low as she walked
through the playground sadly.

On Thursday, Martha woke up feeling Tearful. She didn't want people to make fun of her anymore.

She reached into her drawer and pulled out the most tearful socks she could find. She cried as she pulled them up to her knees.

When she got to school, she noticed that people were pointing and laughing. They thought her mismatched socks were silly.

Martha wasn't sure if she loved her socks anymore. So she didn't walk through the playground proudly that day.

On Friday, Martha woke up
feeling Foolish.

Why would she wear silly socks if people were just going to tease her? She reached into her drawer and pulled out no socks at all. She wasn't going to be laughed at today.

But when she got to school, she noticed that people weren't pointing and laughing at all. What she noticed was something she couldn't believe.
Her entire class - every single student - was wearing mismatched socks.
As Martha stood staring, her teacher came up to her.

"You know, Martha, being different isn't a bad thing," her teacher said. "Look at all of our fun socks!"
Martha's smile grew at the sight of all the mismatched socks. Then, her teacher placed something in her hand - the most colorful, magical, mismatched pair of socks ever!

THE END

CPSIA information can be obtained
at www.ICGtesting.com
Printed in the USA
LVHW071110290922
729561LV00008B/82

9 781649 794789